LOVING
INTERN

WRITERS POUCH

ISBN 979-888555137-3

Aryan P, Prudhvi Kiran P, Vamsi Krishna G, Dinesh S,
Aparajitha A, Varshini K, & Parvati Chintalapati

Contents

Preface

Hello there,

Firstly, I want to thank you for preferring our book. I would like you to know that this book is exceptional as it is written by six writers and every chapter is framed as a short story. Collectively, we have written a story and every writer did their best to narrate to you the tale of a girl. Being the architect of this book, I tried to give you the finest work but if you find any faults, I hope you overlook them. Hope you appreciate our effort and make sure you give us feedback.

- Nikhila Kotni & R. S. Chintalapati

Prologue

Dear Diary,

All of us are destined to have a shoulder to lean on and when the proper occasion comes even the person who spent decades in loneliness would have someone caring for him within days. As fate and time are so alike that both of them are random and relentless, while the first one changes the individual, the second one changes the spirit.

But in my case what transformed me was my sweetheart. Life was so tedious until I met him as an intern. Not that he changed everything but he made me recognize things from a different perception like never before. He motivated me by giving me a target and provoked my determination to such a degree that I reached the pinnacle.

Do you want to know how he inspired me? Well, the answer is just by working in Ratan Industries. To tell you the tale completely, I must tell you a long story but before we get started, I want you to know that today is the most awaited day of my life. It is my first day at Ratan Industries not as an intern any longer but as an employee working in the Heat Exchange Department as an assistant engineer.

I am not just cheerful because my name will be printed in his place or I am not just pleased because I would be sharing a cabin with him. I am happy because I am finally getting to meet my Prince Charming after years.

"I love you!"

- *Naina*

CHAPTER I

Unexpected Start

A few years before

I packed my luggage and boarded a bus to travel to Kochi from Jamalpur. I booked a window seat and after settling down, I recalled my college trip with my friends. The bus conductor distributed water bottles as the bus started.

As the sun rose, I opened the window for fresh air and pulled out my earphones from my handbag. The fact is this is the first time I was travelling alone. The only thought that lingered on my mind was to start my internship as soon as possible as we were already two days late.

I never wanted to be an engineer but as fate always has its way, I had no other choice. I never wanted to do an internship but the curriculum has its way to get things done. As thoughts passed by, I felt the fresh air playing with my hair. The climate was pleasant and I fell asleep quickly.

I got up as the bus driver honked to clear the traffic. I looked out to see that we almost reached Kochi.

I got down at the bus stop and called Meera.

She picked up and said, "Come to the parking lot."

I looked around to find directions and started walking accordingly. When I reached the parking lot, I found her waving at me.

Meera asked, "So did you enjoy the ride?"

I was exhausted and replied, "It was hell as I lacked company!"

She chuckled saying "Don't blame me. Curse yourself, I asked you to come with me yesterday. You were the one who said you needed to spend at least one day with your family."

I replied, "No idiot! My mother would kill me if I left as soon as holidays were declared."

She chuckled and said, "Anyway, I asked my mother to cook chicken. It would be yummy and let's hope for the best tomorrow."

I sat back while she rode the scooter. She is just not a friend like all others but is more like a cousin and I share almost all my secrets with her. I am truly blessed to have her in my life.

After twenty minutes, we reached her place. Her mother stood by the door waiting for us as it was already 9 PM.

As soon as I got down, aunty walked towards me saying, "So you are Naina? Finally, I get to see you after three years. Take your luggage and place them in Meera's room. I will set dinner."

As I walked in, I could see Shiva, Meera's twin brother

playing cricket on his PlayStation. I quickly freshened up and came down to have dinner.

Meera and I started eating and were talking about our internship. Aunty called Shiva to join us and he came after finishing his game. He sat down and looked at me for a moment and kept staring.

Later he introduced himself saying "Hi, I am Shiva. You must be Naina. My sister keeps on telling me about you almost every day when she is here."

I replied, "Nice to meet you, Shiva. What are you doing?"

He stuffed a big chicken piece into his mouth and could not talk clearly. Meera answered sarcastically, "Currently he is completing his MBA and is very talented."

He finally swallowed and attacked saying "Really? At least I know to be punctual unlike you attending your internship days after you were called."

Both of us could not say a word back. Aunty came back from the kitchen and offered more chicken. I refused as I had already eaten too much.

Aunty asked, "How will you do your work at internship if you don't eat good food and stay healthy?"

I just smiled not knowing what to say. We completed our dinner and went to Meera's room. Shiva helped his mother in the kitchen and later brought me an extra pillow and blanket.

Before I thanked him, he left.

We took selfies making weird faces. Meera closed the door and turned on her music player and both of us danced. We also looked into the mirror and felt bad about the pimples and fat. In the end, as always, we spoke about the best qualities we expect our husbands to have. Both of us finally lay on the bed and Meera said, "Finally sleeping at 11 PM after two weeks of end exams. God! Please pass me in the Heat and Mass Transfer exam."

I was too tired to ask for anything and we both fell asleep. Meera woke up at 8 AM, got ready and woke me up. Both of us were ready by 9:30 AM. Reporting was to be done by 10 AM and we started to have our breakfast which was two bread slices.

Meera called Alokya and Neel and they informed us that they would join us at the front gate. Finally, we started and reached Ratan Industries. We were asked by the guards at the entrance to report to Mr Yugandhar.

All the four of us reached Mr Yungandhar's cabin after getting into the main block. A man in his fifties, a bit fat and oily white hair asked us, "So you are the interns who want to join late?"

Meera replied, "Yes sir."

He sternly asked, "Did you guys bring a letter from your principal justifying your reason for the delay?"

I immediately replied, "Do we need that?"

He laughed saying, "Do you think we would let you join late without a valid written reason? You guys can leave. I am sorry but you won't be doing your internship without the letterhead."

I got frustrated as it wasn't our mistake and the company did not mention anything beforehand. I crushed the application form in my hand, out of anger, while Neel, Alokya, and Meera pleaded.

I felt empty and thought it was all over.

CHAPTER II

Love At First Sight?

Dejected after being rejected to work as an intern, all the four of us started walking towards the exit gate.

Just then an idea struck Neel.

"Hey girls, I have a plan which can help us to attend the internship," he said.

"Alright tell us what you have in your mind and please be clear", said Meera as she was both irritated and depressed.

"As we have many of our juniors attending classes since their end exams are not yet done, I'm sure we can obtain a letter attested by our principal through them", assured Neel.

All the six mascara applied eyelashes all of suddenly raised pointing at him, slowly the eyes of the girls lit up.

He continued saying, "We can ask juniors to send us a mail of the scanned copy and produce the letter to the authorities here. And then..."

Before he completed his sentence all the rosy lipstick-smeared lips went berserk shouting, "Our internship isn't cancelled!"

All of us accepted this idea from Neel and appreciated him

for his presence of mind, as he did not wither away under the pressure of rejection. It took us a few hours to get the attested letter from our juniors.

All the smiles were back and everyone was feeling rejuvenated after the events took a turn so rapidly.

Neel submitted the attested letter from our college to Mr Yugandhar, which read that the end exams have been postponed due to some unexpected reasons which led to the delay. Satisfied with the reason provided, Mr Yugandhar gave us a green signal to start our internship in Ratan Industries. All of us were elated and he said "You would start your internship at the Welding Department. Enquire its location and report fast."

We then started walking towards the Welding Department after asking the guards for directions. The path leading to the department was very relaxing and comforting as it had trees on both sides of the footpath providing enough shade.

Overall, the very feeling of finally getting into Ratan Industries was getting on to me. The excitement was creeping into all of us as we entered the Welding Department's administrative office.

Right at the reception, we were greeted with a smile by Mr Ajay Singh.

He said, "So, you are the kids who've come for the internship?"

All of us nodded to which he smiled again.

"Okay, the person you need to meet for today is Mr Vimal Deshpande. You can find him in Room No.13. Please be polite and patient. All the best and I hope you guys have a wonderful time here," he said.

We thanked him for his politeness and moved to Room No.13.

The door to the room was wide open and was inviting people in and God knows what lay in store for us. We were standing just outside the room waiting for permission to enter the room. From the place where we were standing, we could spot a middle-aged man with a clean-shaven face and military hairstyle. He was too busy to even shoot a glance at us. Ten minutes passed by and we were still waiting for his attention.

I was vexed up with the way we were being treated by the officials here. Unable to take it any longer, I knocked on the door and said "Excuse me, sir. We are the students who are to attend the internship in your department from today. Can we please come in?" I completed my long sentence, even though there was a hindrance from my friends about the impatient statement. I felt they were being too idiotic by not seeking permission to get in.

"Oh! Yes, please come in. By the way, what is the duration of your internship here?" he asked immediately without even looking at our faces.

"It's 15 days sir. We would like to acquire knowledge about all the departments in the plant", replied Neel.

"Okay. Don't you think it is a very short period of time to be able to study such a large industry? Anyway, since you've come late to the session today. I got some work to do and would talk to you later. In the meanwhile have a look at the observations and the instruction manuals regarding the Welding Department and its operations and comprehend the uses."

"Yes sir. Thank you", replied Alokya and Meera.

I wasn't that interested in reading the reports. But it wasn't my place to raise a question.

We started reading the reports one after another and they were tiring. We did not expect novels but we did expect them to be a bit interesting. To the mix, all of us were hungry. Just then Mr Ajay Singh came into our room with a smiling face, "Hey kids, still going through the observations! You're doing a wonderful job!" I smirked looking at the report and Meera nudged me, referring that Mr Singh staring at me.

"I know why you guys have grim faces, I understand that you're hungry. Please take a break and get back to the office by 3 PM..." All four of us got up and left the room even before he finished his sentence.

The path to the canteen was on the same road which brought us to the Welding Department but this time, the emotions were different. I was especially very upset with these authorities. It was 2:30 PM and they asked us to be back by 3 PM. They were being too hard on us.

We sat waiting as Neel brought four plates from the counter. Both Meera and Alokya ate a bit and left, vowing not to have lunch at the canteen again. I grabbed my plate and was in a hurry to satisfy my hunger. I was sitting in the place which was opposite to the counter where the food was being served. I happened to see a very thin and lean guy beside the counter checking out on me while I was adjusting my hair. I shrugged him off, completed my lunch and got out of the canteen. It was already 3:05 PM and we hurried back to the department.

We were again greeted by a smiling Singh and just as we entered the cabin of Mr Deshpande, he shouted "What were you doing in the canteen so long? You were late and haven't even completed the work I gave you but you are all enjoying the place right on the first day! I would not appreciate this kind of business. Now, get back to your places and complete the set of files I gave you and give me a report on them in the next one hour!"

All the while, my friends and I trembled with fear due to his sudden outburst. I personally felt very disappointed to be scolded on the first day of our internship. I was aghast at the incident when we entered the room where we were supposed to study the reports. I was literally shouting at my friends. They tried consoling me but I couldn't control my anger. I just did not want to face any more insults.

Stomping out of our room, I knocked on Mr Deshpande's door.

He looked at me and stated, "I've told you to complete the

reports right?”

My friends came following me to the cabin.

“Sir, is there anything you would be teaching us here?” I asked furiously.

“I’ve asked you to complete the reports, first, do the work assigned to you. Then I will try teaching you something”, he said in his usual stern tone.

“What’s the use of going through hundreds of pages of observations, sir? I want you to teach us something about the operations and working of the machines that are used for welding. You aren’t teaching us any of these and you want us to go through those observations without knowing anything about them?”

“What are you going to learn about welding and techniques, you were already taught about those in your curriculum right?”

“What was taught is theory. What’s the use of coming here if you don’t teach us anything practical?” I replied and left the room in a flash, hating to continue the conversation any longer.

I got mad as things were going out of my control. Just when I was passing through Mr Singh’s desk, I saw a person standing before the Welding Department in his mid-twenties probably, tall and bulky with a perfect jawline. He is beyond film stars and is in an entirely different league of beauty.

I was in a trance checking out this mighty and muscular roman figured guy, the smile on his face was like an ornament to a woman's bare neck. The surroundings suddenly became magical and then... SNAP!

I was brought back to my senses by Mr Ajay Singh's words "Cool it down. It's always like this with Mr Vimal. Don't you worry as I have arranged a meeting for you to meet Mr Pratap in the Shells Department tomorrow early in the morning."

I did not hear a word of what Mr Ajay Singh said. I asked myself "Is this magic something called Love? Well, only God knows."

Alokya looked at me closely and immediately asked, "Are you blushing?"

Understanding that I would get caught, I walked out at once. My friends came running after me after they thanked Mr Singh again.

CHAPTER III

Intern'al Blush

All my way back home I was lost in thoughts. I kept asking myself "Is this because I haven't had one guy who is as handsome as he is?"

Nothing seems to bother me, neither the barking Pomeranian nor the whistle of the pressure cooker. I took a shower and when I returned.

Meera asked, snapping her fingers twice "Sweetie, what is wrong with you?"

"Well! Nothing! Why do you ask?" I replied.

"Are you hypnotized?"

For some reason, I did not like her to intervene in my dreams, at least not yet.

"What's the matter Meera?" I asked her absently.

"I never knew all these years that you would take a bath with your clothes on," she retorted.

It might sound pretty strange but that is what I just did. I was daydreaming and was so immersed that I didn't even care to observe.

Another question that I kept asking myself since I saw him

was what this feeling is. "Is it love? Or is it infatuation? To the least, is it an attraction?"

We went down after a few hours to have our supper and when we came back I took my diary and headed to the balcony and sat in the rocking chair enjoying the night lightened by moonlight.

I took a huge breath, awakening my senses. I opened my diary and read the first page

"For the two souls shall be one under the graces of the eternal moon while the waves cleanse our thoughts and the air thickens our affection. For two shall be one ever after and they shall always be united."

I loved poetry and wrote a diary whenever I felt intense feelings pouring out of my mind as I strongly believe thoughts are what define us. I opened a new page and wrote with my black ink pen as always

"Love has never been as dominant on me as it has been today and thoughts have never been so confusing. I know I am dumb and I know no one could be more foolish than I am as I really don't know the difference between infatuation and attraction nor do I know if they are both the same. But I know one thing, from this moment, He is mine. No matter what, He is mine and nothing would please me more than me being His."

I stopped for a moment and wondered if he would accept me. Fear overcame me as I thought if I would be heartbroken and days would turn so bad that I would embrace the darkness. I prayed that there should not be such a day.

I let the clock tick away for the next 6 hours as I dozed off in the rocking chair.

I woke up to the gentle red rays with mild heat in the early hours of the day. I immediately called Neel.

He attended the call asking drowsily "Hello… What's the matter, Naina?"

"The Sun is radiant and looks like he is just waiting for your click. Wake up and capture him before he goes wild." I exclaimed.

"Dolly (his girlfriend) just called me and told the same thing to Naina… So I took some snaps and just fell asleep… Please do not disturb" saying that he cut the call.

I thought "Dolly would not let him lay down even for a moment."

After some time I woke Meera at 7:30 AM. I got dressed in a white kurta with a peacock blue edged border compensating it with a peacock blue dupatta. I added my own touch of beauty to my face with kajal to my blue eyes and wore bangles and nice gold jhumkas.

We started afresh day and all four of us went to the Shell

Department as we had to meet Mr Pratap. As I walked in I was awestruck.

How could the day be any better? As I saw my Prince Charming speaking with Mr Pratap and my eyes moved all around but came back to the same point again and again.

"Firstly welcome to Ratan Industries. I am Pratap Malhotra and let's tour around the Shells Department which is one of the many vital departments" said Mr Pratap after he was done speaking to him.

'Sir, what are the tasks done in this department?" Neel asked as we walked.

It was a huge workshop area under one roof. Most of the people were in orange dresses with fluorescent strips while some of them were in formals with either white or blue caps. I think colour represents their ranking.

I felt every mechanical engineer must visit this place as nothing is more motivating than getting to know what we study in implementation.

"This is huge," said Alokya in awe.

"Oh yes. Everyone in my village can be accommodated here. If I am right, there would be a lot of space left" said Neel, glancing at the infrastructure.

"This is the complete Production Department to be more precise and it is the heart of the industry and the end products are manufactured here" stated Mr Pratap as we walked.

Alarms signalled the timings while most workers drained their energy continuously working. Mr Pratap explained so fabulously that time passed off without notice.

Neel and I headed to the canteen to have meals in the lush green pathway while Alokya and Meera stayed back in the department to have their breakfast as they hated the canteen food the first day.

As he ate, Neel could see me immersed in thoughts "You look disturbed?" he asked.

"Disturbed? Hell no! Why would I be disturbed?" I defended myself.

"Well, your answer tells me that you are. Let me know if I can help you," he assured.

I just nodded my head. I noticed this weird guy who was a thin and fair guy with a shaved head, staring at me just like yesterday. I continued my lunch without bothering him.

We spent the next few hours talking to Mr Pratap about the department and took a tour observing standing beside the employees.

We reached home by 5 o'clock in the evening. I loved Meera's family pretty well as everything went on time, unlike mine. We had supper and Meera left with her mother for some groceries. I sat in the rocking chair again going through my WhatsApp chats and Facebook news feed. I thought of writing my diary but fell asleep.

Day 3: Dear Diary,
Everywhere I go the first thing I do is search for him. But my
Prince Charming is nowhere to be found. Still had fun!

Day 4: Dear Diary,
Interacted with Mr Pankaj in the Press Shop and his
communication skills were terrible. There wasn't a moment we
did not enjoy when he spoke in order to explain the machines
in the shop. Finally, still could not find him.

Day 6: Dear Diary,
Our tour in the Production Department which Mr Pratap
wanted us to visit is almost coming to an end and I am still
not able to see Mr Handsome. I am starting to wonder if he
is really an employee as the more departments we visit he is
nowhere to be found.

Day 9: Dear Diary,
I have never been stalked in my life. This weird guy (weirdo)
is basically stalking me every day during lunch. Nothing ever
bothered me except him. I wish this internship comes to an
end as neither my heart nor my thoughts are peaceful. I will
be meeting Mr Pratap tomorrow asking him about our plan
ahead.

"Sir, can I come in?" I asked knocking on the door.

"Yes. Naina! Come in. Do you look excited today? I like it.
So tell me how your tour in the Production House is going?"

Mr Pratap asked.

"We've almost finished visiting all the departments' sir. So what do we do next sir?"

He curiously asked, "Did you guys go to the Heat Exchangers Department?"

I said, "We didn't sir."

"Well, visit it tomorrow and meet me later."

He got back to his work as I walked out and told others what he told me. We went home early and I watched Frozen that afternoon.

The next day we all directly went to the Heat Exchangers Department and boom there he is, my prince. I was as ugly as possible and cursed myself for not getting ready properly as I almost gave up on meeting him again.

He was wearing a light blue shirt over black pants. He enhanced this attire with nicely trimmed facial hair along his strong jawline. He wore a fat metal wristwatch that was barely visible and his face held a charming smile.

He explained to us everything and not a word went into my head. I kept watching him and time faded like never before. His silky hair and sweet voice held my heart and I was now his captive bound by love. That afternoon Neel and I went to lunch as usual.

Weirdo again stared at me and this time after we started

eating he walked to me and sat beside my chair. Without a word of introduction or anything else this thin pale guy softly said "Naina, I love you."

Neel froze for a moment as that was the worst of all proposals he ever heard. I immediately shouted "No!"

He right away foolishly asked, "Why?"

I did not know why I had to answer him but I held Neel's hand and said "He is my boyfriend. Brace yourself as he is about to punch you so hard that you are never ever again going to take a step forward to propose or at least follow girls for days, intimidating them like hell!"

As I finished, Neel played along by hitting him so hard in the fact that he crashed on the table.

CHAPTER IV

Adios!

That afternoon we spent reading reports as sir was busy guiding workers. I told Meera how Neel hit the weirdo and as usual Alokya did not pay much attention. When we reached home, I sat in my rocking chair and started writing as my thoughts were overflowing. I took a fresh new page and wrote

Dear Diary,
Why am I secretly biting my lower lip when I think about him?
Why is that I am immersed in ecstasy when he is around?
Why is it that I imagine him to be my prince?
Why do I feel his blue eyes as my paradise?
Well, the only thought I get when I close my eyes is both of us running on the shore while the sun's races to rejuvenate us and I embrace him after I get tired.
He is the one I never expected to have as my partner but life never seemed more simple and beautiful.
Prince Charming, I love you!

I thought of weirdo and felt content as he got his shot.

The next morning, I woke up early thrilled and got ready while Meera was still asleep. Later when she woke up, she was shocked to see me ready.

As we reached the Heat Exchangers Department, my eyes were set on him as they always cherished looking at him in his new attire every day. He greeted us and continued explaining where he stopped yesterday.

His audacity and tranquil voice were a big part of his charming beauty. His elegant clothing always made him appear younger. I was so lost in observing that I could not see Meera staring at me.

That evening Meera asked "Naina, why were you staring at sir? What is going on?"

I blushed and she saw me and furiously said "So what I expected is true. Explain to me how it is that someone you've known for days means so much to you?"

"Love at first sight!" I replied.

She did not seem convinced and so I continued saying "I never knew what love meant until I saw him for the first time. It was an avalanche of affection and nothing attracted me like this ever before. Meera, I finally found my eternal lover."

Meera shouted, "You are being insane!"

I looked at her furiously and she continued saying "I am sorry for saying this but what is the difference between you and that weirdo? He stalked you and you stalked sir. If you feel that weirdo deserves a beating for what he did to you, so do you, as you are no different from him."

I shouted "What? Stop!" as I could not defend myself. She still continued firmly "I must say that weirdo was at least good at stalking as he knew where to find you but you don't even know one detail about the sir. You call him your eternal love and you don't even know his name."

I wanted to argue against it but what could I say, she was goddamn right. All my days as an intern, I searched for him in every department and I don't even know any detail of him.

She completed by saying "Naina, I am sorry if I hurt you but don't cover up your lunacy by adding cheesy words like the eternal lover and love at first sight. Our mind is a mad monkey, so don't hang on to it as life will become aimless."

She walked back to the door and just before she left she said "One last thing and make sure you write this in your fancy diary. Stories with hard truths are always classics not because they are mostly tragedies but because they teach you real-life, unlike your fantasies where you run on the beach shores finally falling in your eternal lover's arms, kissing him."

She smashed the door while she left. I sat silent. Even though every word she spoke was hurting, I could not blame her as it takes a lot of courage to tell the truth and live up to it. I looked at the serene blue sky sitting in the rocking chair and after a few moments I finally made up my mind to leave my fate to destiny as most of us do when we end up having no ideas.

I did not want to meet my Prince Charming personally as I felt I might create a bad impression the same way the weirdo did. I opened my diary and wrote on a fresh new page "Adios!" and for the first time, I have written a poem that was so deep and intense.

A spirit is kindled within my body,
Long in waiting with an earnest hope
Both deep and superficial at once,
It shakes me from my slumber of reality.

I become the tiny speck of dust,
Dancing in the beam of sunlight
I become the wave of the ocean that,
Pounds its forceful fist on the shore

I turn into the nonchalant rain cloud,
Teasing all the lands with its shadow
I drift along with the lightest of feathers,
And drop down with melting snowflakes.

Until sober voice echoes in my head
Chiding me to steady my wandering heart
But who doesn't fall for unbridled happiness
And the love I feel when I think about you!

How would you feel when I tell you this?
The force of it hits me hard at my insides
Doubt and fear interlace with my thoughts
I wait like moonlight stopped in its tracks,
Ready to take flight with a leap of faith
Across the darkest stretches of the night
Leaving all the questions for time to answer

- Your loving Intern

I tore off the page and wanted to place it in his cabin without anyone noticing me. The next day while all others wrote the final report, I walked to the Heat Exchangers Department, asked an attendant the location of the Assistant Engineer cabin. He told me sir wasn't in his cabin but I told him I would wait for him.

He pointed out the direction and I was lucky as no one was around. I checked twice and walked into the place of the letter in his office diary that lay on the table.

Calmly I placed it and I saw his nameplate and it read "Nihal Nair, Assistant Engineer". I felt very happy as both of our names started with N and left immediately. While I walked back I saw a thin lean woman wearing a blue saree walking in.

That afternoon we submitted our report to Mr Deshpande and since all of us completed the report I left early that evening as others assured me that they would collect my certificate.

I rushed back to Meera's house, freshened up and had my dinner a bit early and packed my bag. Before I left, I went to aunty and told her "I haven't felt my mother's absence or starvation at any moment. Thank you for taking such good care of me" and aunty invited me to come back next vacation for sure.

Shiva stood beside his mother and I told him "Thank you for the blanket and pillow."

Both of us smiled. Meera dropped me in the bus complex and apologized saying "I am sorry Naina if I hurt you but I want you to stay happy. I hope you understand that I was trying to help you."

I hugged her and got on the bus. When the bus started I recalled memories about the internship and opened my handbag to take out my diary. I could not find it and I was sure I had placed it in my bag. I instantly called Meera to check if I left it in her room in my hurry.

She said it was on the table beside the rocking chair and giggled. I told her to bring it back when she is coming back to college.

CHAPTER V

Now or Never

I badly missed my diary as I wanted to scribble that I am no weirdo. The next morning I reached my home and while I rang the calling bell I said to myself, "Home Sweet Home!"

My mom opened the door and I hugged her as soon as she opened the door. She embraced me back and with a cheerful smile, she said "You have become pale and thin. Anyway, I have a surprise for you waiting in your room."

I left my bags immediately and as I walked in, I asked "What is it?"

When I opened the door I could see my cousin Manisha waiting for me.

I screamed her name and both of us hugged. She said "Finally after a year, I get to see you. How did your internship go?"

The smile on my face faded and my mother rushed me to freshen up and then talk. I gave her my laptop and Wi-Fi password to kill time.

Though Manisha is just my cousin, we are more like twins, maybe because we're born on the same day and year. We are telepathic and are best friends since schooling.

When I was back, she was on my bed watching Cinderella

and I lay beside her and both of us watched the movie. No matter how many times I watched it, Cinderella always makes me smile and maybe that's the reason why I call my Nihal as Prince Charming.

After the movie was done both of us had our lunch and lay on my bed. She slept beside me laying her head on my tummy and looking straight into my eyes she asked "What happened in the internship?"

I calmly narrated to her from the first moment when everything started. I told her how Meera pointed out the facts and how I ended up writing just a poem leaving everything to destiny.

She said hearing about Meera "That girl is a jewel, let her go and you would ruin your life."

I replied, "Tell me something that I don't know."

She instantly said "That something that you don't know is you can't just leave all baffling problems to your destiny and expect life to be cheerful. You must contribute to it as well."

I looked confused and she smiled and continued saying "Look Naina, till now you've been chilling and enjoying your life. We all have enjoyed it quite a lot. However, there would be a time in everyone's life when they must push themselves to be someone who they weren't ever before."

I shouted "Come on! What do you want me to do?"

She pleasantly answered, "If you are serious about him, it's time you get serious about your life too."

I asked again, "How me being serious is going to help me meet my Nihal?"

"I have friends who have left their relationships and wept for days, unable to stay strong with determination and compassion. If you want to tell me you love him, tell me when you win his heart, if you want to prove to Meera that you are not a weirdo, prove it by loving him after you know him by heart and soul, ultimately if you want him to be your eternal love? Stop thinking that it is all over and start over. As your journey has just begun and no matter what, never let it go. Trust me, your prince is going to come back and destiny shall only help those who step forward. Adios? This is just the beginning." She boldly said.

My mom suddenly opened the door and told Manisha that her father was waiting for her. Before she left, she said one last thing "Now or never!"

She left without saying a word and I immediately wanted to take a book and write what she just said but I felt I would never forget them.

CHAPTER VI

The Trio

Desire is one emotion that is unquenchable and the more you seek the more it enhances. For almost two years, I tried getting a job in Ratan Industries and nothing felt more challenging. Finally, in my second attempt, I got employed. I felt my hard work paid off when I was posted in the Heat Exchangers Department as an Assistant Engineer and like Manisha believed destiny did lend its support.

When I reached the industry, the guards pointed me in the direction and asked me to report to Mr Nihal Nair taking a look at my joining letter. As I reached the department, I went straight to the Deputy Engineer's cabin and knocked on the door.

While my heartbeat paced, my eyes waited to feast on his charm. I heard him finally say politely "Come in" and nothing felt more beautiful in years.

As I walked in, I could see him more ravishing than ever with his soul patch beard style. He has become a bit lean but more dynamic and his words were honey-sweet. He requested me to have a seat.

I gave him my reporting form and other requested documents. As soon as he took them he stared at me in amazement. I wanted to tell him that I had interned here but he stood up and asked me to follow.

Both of us reached his previous cabin and he said "Your profile says you have previously interned here. So I don't think you would need a lot of help. Anyway, let me know if you need anything."

I walked into the cabin, sat in his chair and it felt more empowering. Two years of effort and two motivating friends is all it took me to come back and meet my sweetheart. I worked for a few hours and all of a sudden; Nihal opened my door shouting "Oh! Alluring star! Let's go have lunch!"

On our way to the canteen, he observed me thinking about what he called me and explained "I am a big fan of poetry and call my friends by the meaning of their names. Your name means beautiful eyes so alluring star."

As we reached the canteen, Nihal introduced me to Mr Vivek, his close friend who worked in the Welding Department. Truth be told, he was amazingly beautiful, a lot better than Nihal I felt.

Black silky hair, greyish black eyes and milk-white skin tone with a stiff body and confident personality. Tell me what could any girl want more?

Every day all the three of us had our lunch together. Vivek and I loved William Blake's works especially the poem "Marriage of Heaven and Hell" fascinated both of us and one of the most spoken topics by all the three of us was poetry.

As weeks passed by, I started to know more about Nihal.

He is hilarious, philosophical and resolute at work. His unending energy and passion for learning were his most redeeming qualities.

One day after we had our lunch and Vivek left for the Welding Department, Nihal asked me to come to his cabin and I went. As soon as I entered the requested "Naina since you love poetry, I would like to show you a poem I received from an intern a few years back. I hope it is a girl and tell me how it is."

Saying this he passed me a folded paper. As I unfolded it, I could observe it was torn from a diary and with black ink, the first line beside the date read "Adios". It made me recollect my last day of internship again.

He enthusiastically exclaimed "Naina! Read the verses, aren't they heart touching? These verses are true feelings and this is magnificent poetry. Both of us know the right-hand thumb rule that says fine verses are always written in grief."

I started blushing and he softly whispered while walking near me "Nothing would please me more if this was written by my girlfriend."

My internal voice shouted "Go on! Tell him it is you!" but I couldn't. I felt I must tell him the full story soon and made up my mind to propose to him in the days to come, finally making my Prince Charming mine forever.

CHAPTER VII

A Heart-breaking Handshake

A week passed by and my thoughts about conveying my love kept delaying every day. Every time I saw him, I wanted to reveal that I am his mysterious poet and lover, but for some reason, I waited for the perfect time.

Every day I adored the moments when he applauded the poem and spoke about me naively not knowing that it was me.

Whenever he talked about the poem, I documented his compliments in my diary. For me, they were all memories of love given by him honestly. A week later I finally made up my mind to propose to him on the coming Friday. I spent the previous night worrying about his reply.

The next day I arrived late to the office as I took a lot of time getting ready. As I paced forward hurriedly, I saw a bike stopped beside me. After the driver took off his helmet and adjusted his silky hair I could see Vivek.

He immediately said "Get on the bike. We are getting late to sign in and there is a long way to go."

I got on to his bike and he raced forward. Both of us signed in for the morning shift and were on our way back to our departments while I was about to thank him.

He asked "Naina, I wanted to ask you if you could join me

for dinner?”

I looked at him in astonishment and the next thing he did was walk to his department whistling.

That morning Nihal assisted me in updating office files and as we worked I had the pleasure of touching his smooth skin for the first time and surprisingly he was very warm.

That afternoon while we had our lunch Vivek asked me “By the way Naina, did you love anyone in the past?”

I stopped eating for a moment and I could see a cute dimple on Nihal’s face.

I looked into Nihal’s eyes and answered “Yes I did and I am still committed to him. Fun fact is my love is what brought me here in the first place.”

Vivek raised his eyebrows and sarcastically exclaimed “Impelling and immersing love.” and laughed loudly. Nihal also smiled and suddenly out of nowhere Mr Deshpande arrived and grabbed a chair towards our table and sat between me and Nihal. He greeted everyone with a smile and his entry chucked our conversation.

Vivek formally said “Hello sir” and as usual, Mr Deshpande did not care to reply. He turned towards Nihal and started speaking to him while Vivek turned to me and whispered “He talks so formally with Nihal as he is a deputy and doesn’t even care to value me as I am his assistant. Jackass!”

I giggled and thought “Lucky me.” A few moments later

Nihal said "It's time" and all of us started back. Both of them came along with us to Heat Exchangers Department.

I got annoyed as that afternoon I wanted to propose to Nihal and I got depressed as I could not find a private moment thereby leaving me unfruitful on the day's intention. All of us walked into our department and as soon as we entered, a girl with a shining black side braided hairstyle, milk-white skin tone, and thin personality waited for us. One word to describe her is exquisite.

As soon as she saw Vivek, she raced towards and hugged him. Later she shook hands with Deshpande.

For a moment she looked at Nihal and even hugged him.

"My goodness, who is she? How come all of them know except me about her?" I thought and was about to ask Vivek, at that very moment Nihal turned to me and said "Naina, I want you to meet Priyanka."

She hastily extended her hand to shake hands and to her left hand, I could see a golden ring. While I extended my hand Nihal continued saying "My fiancé."

And now I could see diamonds on the golden ring which read "N" and for the first time I looked at Nihal's hand and he had the same style ring that reads "P".

I stood still, heartbroken and could not feel my senses. My spine chilled with fear and within no time loneliness embraced me. I silently left with a smile on my face.

CHAPTER VIII

The Tale of A Reckless Man

Dear Diary,
What is more painful than death? Well, the answer is being
forgotten by your friends as if we did not exist and what is
more painful than getting rejected by your loved one?
Watching them embrace others right before you not knowing
they are being loved by you.

I wrote and sat silent all afternoon in my cabin and made
sure I did not cry. That evening when I reached home I
went straight to my room and slept on my bed. I recalled
the numerous days I dreamed of getting into his arms and
tears started to flow down.

My mother saw me crying. She came near me while I wiped
my tears and sat beside me on my bed. She tenderly asked,
"Did your Prince Charming say no?"

I held her and started crying out loud and she said "Didn't
you ever know that I read your diary?"

I did not reply but moved, placing my head on her lap
and closing my eyes. She placed her hand on my head and
told me "Not very long ago there was a boy who lived in
a small town. He was handsome and decent; he adored his
mother as she pampered him but he dreaded his father.
This beautiful boy loved a gorgeous girl with all his heart
and she loved him back. Both of them spent days under the
shining stars and one day when the boy came back home

his father summoned him and told him that he wanted to get him married.

The boy never spoke against his father but for the first time, he wanted to oppose but he couldn't because of his fear. He married another girl, shattering his heart and making himself a man and his wife a woman. For two years everything went well and both of them were blessed with a beautiful daughter. But after two years the man's father died suddenly and that very same year he met his eternal lover back. One day the man came home with a lot of money and gave it to his wife. He told her the truth and told her to take good care of his daughter. His wife pleaded with him not to go. She asked him to stay back for her daughter at least but lust drove him so mad that he didn't stop even after looking at his daughter."

I could feel drops falling on my forehead and I opened my eyes to see my mother cry. In a broken voice, she said "The wife at last said if you have made up your mind to leave, never ever return no matter what. From that day on, the woman was all by herself."

I sat and asked my mother "Why are you crying now? Why do you even care if a reckless man made a mistake?"

My mother smirked and replied "Because the reckless man in the story is your father, the woman who pleaded was me and the girl born was you. For years, I have never told you this because I feel bad for marrying such a worthless man immersed in lust that he doesn't even care to take responsibility. I felt bad because the only man I ever loved was him and he let go of me for another woman as if I didn't matter."

I was shocked and curiously asked "How did you grow back strong? How did you overcome your loneliness?"

She answered, "You. It was you who brought me back. One night I recalled your father and started crying. You were three years old and were sleeping beside me. You woke up hearing me and with your cute little hands, you tried wiping my tears. Nothing felt more comforting and I decided to never cry again because I had a soul caring for me. My father, husband, friends all abandoned me and I thought there wasn't a soul that cared for me and when I heard you say in a cute voice "Don't cry, mama." I knew I had you and no matter what I had to take care of you."

I hugged her tight and she whispered "We all are stuck with sadness because we always seek what we don't have but we would let go of all those who love us as we are foolish and adamant."

She continued by saying "What I have learnt in life is every cloud has a silver lining and every mistake has its payback. Accomplish good deeds, trust in your relations, love without desires and life would be bliss."

Wiping her tears, a moment later she left. I laid back on the bed and my phone buzzed and it was Vivek. As soon I attended the call "Are you alright? Why did you leave without even meeting me this evening as always?" he asked.

His concern was overwhelming and I told him "I am ready to go to dinner with you!"

CHAPTER IX

Date With Karma

I asked myself why I agreed to have dinner with Vivek. Well, I don't know. Maybe it was because I was ignored by Nihal and felt that Vivek was worth my time. I've never been in such a situation and the only thing my internal voice kept saying was "Get out of this!" but I couldn't help myself at least now.

All my thoughts were interrupted when my phone vibrated and the screen showed Vivek's name on it.

"Hey, have you even started? I'm already waiting for you. Trust me this moment would be memorable." said Vivek trying to lighten up things as he already knew that I was upset.

"I am almost there," I replied.

He cut the call and I felt there wouldn't be a girl who would not be impressed if a boy shows concern and perhaps, in my opinion, it is the best way to impress.

The moment I stepped out of the cab, I was greeted by a beaming Vivek who put out his hand in order to hold mine. I readily handed over mine and felt very cosy around him. He held the door open, welcomed me inside and then he got into the restaurant. And before I could decide about the chair, he pulled out the chair, gestured to me to have my seat, made me feel comfortable and then pushed it a little towards the table which was a bit higher for someone like me to be comfortable with.

All the things he is doing and the way he is looking after me was actually making me passionate. I felt my future with Nihal was something that would never ever happen. The change in Vivek's behaviour, the smartness and the etiquette he's been showering were exquisite. I've never felt this affection from a guy and the best thing is he is someone I have been working with and this drew me more towards him.

After a few moments, both of us settled and he curiously asked "Now, tell me Naina. Who is that guy of yours? Tell me madam, who is that lucky guy to earn your commitment?"

I lied by replying "No, Vivek. I've bluffed. There's no one and I'm still in pursuit to find my dream guy. Looks like I am unfortunate as I could not find mine. Whereas all the others are just enjoying every moment with their loved ones and seriously I am very frustrated."

Vivek wickedly smiled and comforted me by saying "Oh. Never mind buddy. You will definitely find someone who will blow your brains out. I am sure you will find him very soon."

Never in my mind did I ever think of Vivek but now everything he said felt beautiful. I am very much under his influence unknowingly. I felt his words pleasing and felt him as a comfortable partner. Because all I ever wanted is someone to be there for me no matter what.

However, I didn't brush away from the thought of getting into a relationship with him. I just wanted to be sure as I did not want to end up like in my previous relationship. So I immediately asked "What about you Vivek? You don't have a girlfriend?"

I was expecting a no and he answered saying "No, I'm just like you, looking for a perfect partner in life."

These words reverberated for a few moments and I felt like there's no one happier than me in the world.

I made up my mind, took three deep breaths and faintly said "Vivek, I have wanted to tell you this for a long time and it's kind of tough for me to actually reveal the fact that I've fallen in love with you lately. The only person who can take care of me more than myself would be you and I want you to be part of my life till the very last breath of mine."

I paused for a moment and asked, "Are you feeling the same about me?"

Before he even responded, I felt relieved as I had finally spoken my heart out.

The answer was yet to come and Vivek was lost in his thoughts and was just staring at the ceiling. I could observe his attitude change and pride adorned his face at that very moment.

He asked me, "Naina, I would like to ask you a question. Would you prefer a guy with an ugly face with a noble heart or a fair guy with a dirty mind?"

The question seemed tricky and the doubts that loomed over why he asked me the question were increasing.

"Of course, I would go with someone who has a noble heart no matter how he looks."

He smiled and cunningly said "Do you think for at least one moment that I would believe that you would prefer a noble heart? Tell me what you did, when a boy with a noble heart walked to you and proposed?"

I did not get him and asked, "Who?"

He faintly said "A guy with a shaved head and thin as a stick. Years back came to you and proposed. What did you do then?"

I got confused and asked "Weirdo?" and for the first time in years, I remembered him and could see Vivek a little bit like him.

He immediately shouted "Yes! I am that weirdo! I've been waiting for this very moment for so long. I wanted you to propose to me after you lose your long time lover Nihal. The cute and perfect jaw lined Assistant Engineer had already got engaged with a perfectly beautiful girl who is a lot better than you. I knew that your dreams would be shattered when he introduced his fiancé and I was waiting to rejoice to see him do it."

I ran out of words and taking back what was said cannot

be done. I understood that Vivek had a vile nature and was waiting for me to self-destruct myself. I couldn't let my tears out and was furious with myself.

He burst into laughter saying again "You know what? I really enjoyed it when Priyanka shook hands with you."

He continued saying "Nothing felt happier as you were getting your heart thrashed in front of someone you loved. You surely deserved that. You bitch! Now go fuck yourself and if you even have the slightest of emotions left in you, go look at your pathetic self in the mirror and reconsider all your decisions. Adios!"

He stormed out with a beaming face as my internal self kept telling "What goes around always comes around."

CHAPTER X

The Promise

I reached back home and all along my way back I regretted it as I could have just said to him a few years ago but I made a fuss and as expected karma is inevitable.

I had no more strength left in me and lying on the bed I fell asleep. The next being Saturday, I killed time by watching Korean shows. In the evening while I was sitting on my balcony reading "Treasure Island" for the third time, a car stopped before my gate.

Nihal got down and came near me and asked, "Are you free now?"

Though I was angry with him and wanted to say no. I teased him by asking "Yes. What is the matter? Should I select a good dress for your mistress?"

He said, "I'll give you 5 minutes to get ready and come with me."

I did not ask him anything else and both of us got into the car. The climate was fantastic as the cool breeze whispered in our ears the tunes sung by nature and the beach waves drummed by crashing themselves onto the stones. He forwarded his hand and I placed my hand in his.

Both of us walked near to the shore and sat on a stone on the sand. The waves touched our feet while the moonlight rejuvenated our energy.

Nihal looked straight into my eyes and asked "This is what you wanted right? Sitting near the seashore enlightened by moonlight and sanctified with a breeze while the waves wash away your sins?"

He calmly said, "When the two souls shall become one."

I was surprised as that is what is written on the first page of my diary. He explained "Naina I want to tell you what has happened and it all started two months before your internship with my engagement with Priyanka. When you were doing your internship, I did not know that you had feelings for me or else I would have cut it off back then but after you left, your friend Meera came to me and gave me your diary and told me that she made her brother take your diary out of your bag so that she could give it to me. I was amazed to see you adore me so much without even knowing me for real. I loved being called Prince Charming and I read your diary as being loved is the best of all feelings. I gave it back to Meera when she left for college and thought it was all over because you would never be coming back. But let me tell you seriously, your determination is quite impressive and when I read your name the day you gave me your joining letter, I was awestruck. I was still confused about if you loved me or not and wanted to know if you really still did and so I gave you your poem. However, you did not at least reveal that it was you who wrote it. I thought maybe it is all for the good and introduced you to my fiancé, trusting that you did not have feelings for me. But when Priyanka saw you when both of you were shaking hands, I got bashed by her that very afternoon because she could see the sheer pain in your eyes. She told me why she hastily shook hands because she could see your heart shattered and that is the reason why I am here. She knows the pain by experience and is concerned for you. She was the first person to read your poem and felt so happy that you loved me deeply that she came to me with your poem."

I understood that the thin lean woman in the blue saree who walked in after I left Nihal's cabin placing my poem was Priyanka. Everything said was a shock to me and I had nothing to say back.

He continued saying "I am sorry for hurting you and it was never my intention. I am not going to tell you that you would get a better man as I leave that to fate but I will promise you this."

Saying this he took my right hand in between both his hands and said "I might not be the man whom you wanted me to be and I might not be the man who will share a life with you but I will be the man who you can look up to share your grief. I promise you to stand by your side in all your problems, to protect yourself and always ensure that you are happy. Well, this is all that your Prince Charming can do. Since you wanted me to be your eternal love, I shall be it by promising you this."

I hugged him as he said "To be loved is cheerful but to love is bliss. I am cheerful that you found your happiness in me and I promise I would live up to it and you my dear will always be my loving Intern."

Saying this he kissed my forehead and it was one of the most memorable moments in my life.

A moment later, he stood up and asked me "Let's go?"

I wanted to take my own time and said "I will stay for some time and then go."

While he walked back I called him and told him "You did not have to do this but you did. Thank you for trying to help me come back."

He smiled and walked back towards the car.

Priyanka stood leaning on the car and cheerfully said "That is my Nihal. I am happy that you did it for me. I hope she finds a good person."

Nihal replied "She will and I will make sure she will. I will always live up to the promise I just made."

Epilogue

Twenty Years Later

"That is my story, son. Now before you judge, I would like you to know that I was foolish, adamant and ignorant. To date, I don't even know why I proposed to Vivek and the least explanation I tell myself every time when I think about it is that I was in pain and expected support. I don't know what made me like Nihal so much that he was the cause for my determination and I also don't even know how I stood strong when he just walked away promising me nothing but support." I said straight into my son's olive-green eyes.

It has been an hour since we arrived and my daughter and husband were enjoying the waves while I sat with my son on the same stone as I sat with Nihal.

I continued "Every night, pillows sunk my tears, faith shattered and heart wept in agony wanting someone to just care. For a year I was not myself but everything would end. There will always be a day in everyone's life when they are left in the void and that day, life is gifting you a second chance. This time, life will ensure that you can utilize it to become someone you are destined to be. You may believe that I was betrayed, insulted or heartbroken but what I believe is that I was foolish enough not to accept the real truth coming racing towards me. Trust me, when I say we must all face the truth and experience all our karma. That day, you would understand that life has many more things than just a soul mate, friends and happiness. It would make you realize that you are meant for something and never fail to strive in order to achieve it."

Vihan asked, "Don't you still love him?"

I said to myself "Yes I do and I will until my last day." But I told him "You would know the answer when you tell your story to your son. Now go play with your sister and stop regretting Tabu and your decision to start a relationship."

He stood up and before he raced forward he said "Mama, the best thing I have heard in your story is when aunt Meera told you that mind is a mad monkey. Perhaps she was right; conceivably we all have failures and are so lost in pain that we don't want to hear anything that ends bitterly."

He continued "I envy you mother, as father adores you and I would be the happiest man if my wife would love me the way he loves you."

I smiled and replied "She will. Trust me."

As I enjoyed the pleasant climate for a while, Shiva came back and sat beside me. I leaned on his shoulder and he held my hand and while the waves cleansed our thoughts, the air thickened our affection.

We kissed.

About Contributors

1. **Chethana Nagulapalli**
   Contributor of "Unexpected Start" & "The Trio"

   Chethana has been a member of the community since 2015 and she writes flash fiction. Her works can be accessed at writerspouch.com/profile/23

2. **Mounika Kodeboina**
   Contributor of "Adios!"

   Mounika has been a member of the community since 2014 and she writes experiences and flash fiction. Her works can be accessed at writerspouch.com/profile/12

3. **Nikhila Kotni**
   Creator of "Loving Intern" & Contributor of "Lost City"

   Nikhila has been a member of the community since 2014 and she writes flash fiction, short stories & poems. Her works can be accessed at writerspouch.com/profile/6

4. **Priyanka Udatha**
   Contributor of "A Heart-breaking Handshake"

   Priyanka has been a member of the community since 2015 and she writes flash fiction & short stories. Her works can be accessed at writerspouch.com/profile/16

5. **Rajiv R Nair**
   Contributor of "Love At First Sight?" & Date With Karma"

   Rajiv has been a member of the community since 2015 and he writes flash fiction & short stories. His works can be accessed at writerspouch.com/profile/24

6. **R. S. Chintalapati**
   Creator & Contributor of "Loving Intern"

   Ravi is the founder of the community and he writes short stories & clicks pictures. His works can be accessed at writerspouch.com/profile/2

7. **Santhosh Annabuttla**
   Poet of "Adios!"

   Santhosh has been a member of the community since 2011 and he writes poems. His works can be accessed at writerspouch.com/profile/3

8. **Viswanath Perala**
   Contributor of "Intern'al Blush"

   Viswanath has been a member of the community since 2015 and he writes short stories. His works can be accessed at writerspouch.com/profile/15

About Editors

1. **R. K. Chamarla**

   Raghuveer has been a member of the community since 2011 and he has edited numerous contributors over the years. His edited works can be accessed at writerspouch.com/profile/1

2. **Sameer Ayyagari**

   Sameer has been a member of the community since 2016 and he has edited a couple of contributions. His edited works can be accessed at writerspouch.com/profile/63

About Photographer

Pankaj Tottada

Pankaj has been a member of the community since 2015 and he has contributed numerous photographs. His contributions accessed at writerspouch.com/profile/13

About Community

Writers Pouch is an Indian community that commissions various works of different art forms. Encompassing creators, contributors, editors, proofreaders, reviewers, photographers, and illustrators, the organisation aims to create unique art forms in every genre. Established in 2009, Writers Pouch started publishing short stories,essays and poems. Later on, the organisation even started releasing novelettes, novellas, novels, book series, & non-fiction.

The goal of Writers Pouch is to explore art uniquely, which is accomplished by commissioning a group of artists on every project. They are a home for all creative individuals striving to tell their stories or ideas creatively while holding on to their principles. If you loved our works, visit our website at writerspouch.com to buy our other titles.

1. I'm Your Loving Intern